Text copyright © Kathy Elgin 2001
Illustrations copyright © Tony Morris 2001
Book copyright © Hodder Wayland 2001

Published in Great Britain in 2001
by Hodder Wayland, an imprint of
Hodder Children's Books

Cataloguing in Publication Data
Elgin, Kathy
  Julius Caesar. – (The Shakespeare Collection)
  1. Caesar, Julius, 100 B.C. – 44 B.C. – Juvenile fiction
  2. Children's stories
  I. Title II. Shakespeare, William, 1564–1616. Julius Caesar
  823.9'14 [J]

ISBN: 0 7502 3352 4

Printed in China by WKT

Hodder Children's Books
A division of Hodder Headline Limited
338 Euston Road, London NW1 3BH

The Shakespeare Collection

JULIUS CAESAR

RETOLD BY KATHY ELGIN

Illustrated by Tony Morris

HODDER
Wayland

an imprint of Hodder Children's Books

Character list:

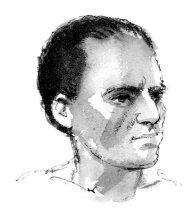

Julius Caesar

Calpurnia

wife of Caesar

Mark Antony

Caesar's general

Octavius Caesar

Caesar's adopted son

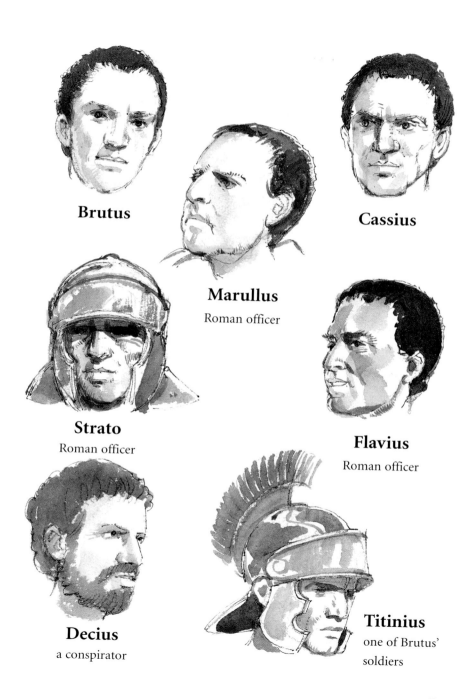

Brutus

Marullus
Roman officer

Cassius

Strato
Roman officer

Flavius
Roman officer

Decius
a conspirator

Titinius
one of Brutus'
soldiers

5

The city of Rome was buzzing with excitement. It was the feast of Lupercal, one of the most important days in the Roman calendar, and the celebration games were about to begin. The whole city was out on the streets. But there was something else going on, too.

Marullus looked suspiciously at a group of men in front of him. "What do you lot think you're doing, out in public in your best clothes and without your union badges? You – what trade are you? And what are you doing here?"

"I'm a cobbler," replied the man. "And we're celebrating Julius Caesar's triumphant return to Rome."

"What *triumph?*" snarled Marullus. "What about Pompey, who used to be such a favourite of yours – have you forgotten him?"

There was a time when the people of Rome would have stood in the street all day just to watch Pompey drive by, and now they were falling over themselves to welcome the man who defeated him!

"You're a fine lot!" shouted Marullus. "Go on, clear off back to your houses."

"They should be ashamed of themselves," muttered Flavius, another officer. "We'd better go and see if they've put decorations on any statues of Caesar for this so-called celebration. If they have, take them down. This Caesar needs to be put in his place before he gets too big for his boots."

In the main square Julius Caesar stood surrounded by a big crowd. He was whispering instructions to Mark Antony, who was favourite to win the races. Antony was Caesar's most trusted general. They had been through many campaigns together and were good friends.

Suddenly, an old man stepped out of the crowd. "Caesar!" he called. "Caesar! Beware the Ides of March!"

"Who said that?" asked Caesar, looking round. But the man had vanished again.

"Never mind him," said Caesar grandly. "Let's get on with the celebrations." And he led the way to where the races were about to take place.

Two men stayed behind.

"Aren't you going to see how the race goes, Brutus?" asked Cassius.

"Not me," replied Brutus. "I'm not the sporty type."

Cassius smiled. "That's good," he said, "because there's something I want to speak to you about..." He was interrupted by a great cheer from the crowd.

"What's happening?" asked Brutus, turning towards the noise. "I hope that doesn't mean they've chosen Caesar as emperor!"

"You're not in favour of that, then?" asked Cassius, casually.

"No," answered Brutus, adding quickly, "although I do respect him. But what's all this about, Cassius? What is it you want to talk to me about?"

Cassius took a deep breath. What he was about to say was dangerous. "It's Caesar," he began. "The people are treating him like a god, but he's just an ordinary man, no better than you or me. In fact, he's worse – once, when he was showing off by challenging me to swim across the river Tiber, he was so feeble I had to rescue him from drowning! And now we're all supposed to let him lord it over us and behave as if we were his subjects. I'd rather be dead than submit to that..." Cassius was becoming more angry as he spoke.

Brutus said nothing.

"What's happened to us Romans, that we've allowed one man to become so powerful?"

Brutus looked grave. He didn't hate Caesar as much as Cassius did, but he knew that what his friend was saying was true. He also knew it was treason and he suspected that Cassius was involved in a plot. Cassius had always been hot-headed and often acted recklessly.

"Cassius, we can't discuss this now – I will consider all you've said and we'll talk again later. But I can tell you this – I'm proud to be a Roman, but I'd rather live in a village than in this city with Caesar in control."

Just then Caesar and his followers arrived back from the games. Seeing Brutus and Cassius together, Caesar muttered to Antony, "I don't trust that Cassius – he's too skinny and he thinks too much. Men like that are dangerous. Come over here and tell me more about him."

Brutus called to another friend, Casca. "What was all the shouting about?" he asked.

Casca snorted. "It was a real pantomime. Mark Antony offered Caesar the emperor's crown and he made a big show of refusing, although you could tell he really wanted it. Three times he did it, pretending to be so modest. It made me laugh. And the crowd got more and more worked up, shouting and throwing their caps in the air. What a performance! I can tell you something else, though – Marullus and Flavius have been sentenced to death for removing the decorations from statues of Caesar."

Brutus and Cassius looked at each other in alarm.

Later, when Cassius was left alone, he smiled to himself. "Brutus, I think you're on our side, but it might take a little more persuasion. A few forged letters should do it. And then watch out, Caesar..."

That night strange sights were seen in Rome. Thunder and lightning raged over the city; a lion prowled the city centre and ghostly men walked the streets. Even worse, a screech-owl had been heard hooting in daylight – a terrible omen. The people were afraid – these things had to be warnings of some great event to come.

Brutus could not sleep. He walked in his orchard, deep in thought. The conversation with Cassius was troubling him. Brutus was an honourable man, and he had no personal grudge against Caesar as Cassius seemed to have, but he could see the danger ahead. Caesar was ambitious and, if he became emperor, he might well turn into a real tyrant. There was only one way to stop Caesar becoming more powerful, and that was to kill him...

Just then a servant came out with a letter. "Sir, I found this by the window, someone must have thrown it in."

Brutus opened the note. It had no signature, but it was the same as others he had found in his house recently, telling him to take action against Caesar:

Yes, he *had* to do something, and soon! Brutus thought about the strange omens, and suddenly he remembered the old man in the crowd earlier. What had he said? "Beware the Ides of March, Caesar." That meant the fifteenth – and that was tomorrow...

A servant interrupted Brutus' thoughts to tell him that Cassius was at the door with some other men. "They've all got their capes pulled down to hide their faces," he said. "They look very suspicious."

"The other conspirators," thought Brutus. "Now I must decide!"

As soon as they came in, Cassius began whispering urgently to Brutus, outlining the plot.

Reluctantly, Brutus agreed to join them. "But let's not swear an oath," he said, "The justice of our cause is enough. An oath would make us seem like criminals."

"I think we should kill Mark Antony, as well," put in Cassius, impetuous as ever. "He could make things difficult for us if we let him live."

But Brutus didn't want any more killing. "Getting rid of Caesar is one thing, but we're not murderers. Anyway, Antony's harmless; what can he do once Caesar's gone?"

Cassius thought of something else. "What if Caesar doesn't go to the Capitol today? You know how superstitious he is. All these strange happenings will have made him nervous."

"Leave it to me," said Decius, one of the other conspirators, "I'll make sure he's there."

Calpurnia, Caesar's wife, was in tears. "All these bad omens!" she wept. "Something terrible is going to happen. Please don't go to the Capitol today. Tell them you're sick and stay at home."

"If I do that they'll think I'm afraid," argued Caesar. But Calpurnia was so upset that in the end he gave in. He was just about to send a message to the Senate when Decius arrived.

"My wife had a bad dream," explained Caesar. "She dreamt that my statue was pouring with blood, and all the Romans washed their hands in it. She doesn't want me to go to the Senate House today, so I've decided not to – will you tell them?"

Decius thought quickly. "But Caesar," he said, laughing, "Calpurnia has got it all wrong. That was a *good* dream. It means that you are like a fountain of life to the people of Rome, they owe you everything. There's nothing to fear – and anyway I have some other news. Today they are going to give you the emperor's crown. If you don't go, they may change their minds. Look, here are Brutus and the others to escort you there."

The plan worked, of course. Caesar put on his cloak and set out for the Capitol.

As usual there was a crowd of men waiting to ask Caesar for favours. He brushed them all aside loftily and to show he had not been frightened by the warning the day before, said loudly, "Well, today is the Ides of March."

"Yes, Caesar," came back a voice from the crowd, "but it's not over yet!"

Cassius and the other conspirators started moving in, slowly surrounding Caesar, while one of them carefully drew Antony to one side.

"I beg you again to let my brother return from exile," began one of the men, but Caesar refused.

When the others repeated the request, Caesar turned on them angrily. "I've made my decision," he said coldly, "and I *never* change my mind."

It was his last act of arrogance.

The conspirators pressed closer, drew their daggers and stabbed Caesar over and over again.

As he fell, he saw that Brutus, his friend, was one of them. "Oh, Brutus," he gasped. "*You, too? Then die, Caesar!*"

Immediately, all the conspirators fell on Caesar's body, dipping their hands in his blood and crying, "Freedom! Liberty! The tyrant is dead!"

There was chaos in the crowd, and while Brutus was trying to calm them, Mark Antony appeared. He looked at the bloody scene but showed no emotion. "Am I next?" he asked. "If so, let's get it over with."

"We have nothing against you, Antony," replied Brutus. "Caesar was my friend, too, but he had to be killed – when I explain it all to you, I'm sure you'll agree."

Antony looked away. Then he asked to be allowed to speak at Caesar's funeral.

Brutus agreed at once, but Cassius whispered urgently, "No, Brutus, don't let him – he might turn the crowd against us."

But Brutus was sure that when he explained the reasons for the assassination to the crowd, they would all understand. "After I've done that, Antony can say a few words," he added, as he and the others left.

"Oh, Caesar," cried Antony as soon as he was alone, "forgive me for seeming to side with your murderers. This was a terrible deed! I will avenge your death, even if it means the whole country will be plunged into war!" And he hurried off to the funeral.

*B*rutus was already on the platform, explaining to the crowd why they had had to kill Caesar. "He wanted all the power for himself, and we couldn't allow that," he was repeating. "Although we all loved him, we love Rome and freedom more. We didn't do this just for ourselves, but for all of you. To prove it, look – here's the dagger I used to kill Caesar. I'd kill myself with it, too, if it would help Rome."

The crowd was convinced. "Brutus, Brutus!" they chanted. "He's saved us from that tyrant Caesar! Let's have Brutus for our leader!"

Satisfied, Brutus left the platform and Antony took his place.

Antony began very respectfully, agreeing with Brutus that tyrants were dangerous and had to be removed. He told them, too, that Brutus was an honourable man and must have acted in good faith. But then he started to remind the crowd of the good things that Caesar had done for Rome.

"Remember all the prisoners he captured, and the fortune we made from their ransoms? That wasn't just for his own good. And don't you remember the other day, when I offered him the crown and he refused it, *three times?* Does that sound like the act of an ambitious man?"

The crowd began muttering. Perhaps Caesar hadn't been so bad after all?

"He's right, you know, about the crown," said some. "Antony's the most honest man in Rome, he wouldn't lie to us."

Brutus and Cassius listened in dismay. This wasn't supposed to happen.

But Antony hadn't finished. He went on with his clever speech. "I don't want to say anything against Brutus and Cassius, they're both honourable men and I'm sure they acted nobly. But look, here is Caesar's will. If you knew what was in it, you'd know how he loved you all."

"Read it!" shouted the crowd. "Let's hear it!"

"No," said Antony, putting the paper away. "It would upset you too much. Who knows what you'd do? I'm sorry, I've said too much already."

"No, read it! Read the will!" yelled the crowd,
working themselves up into a frenzy. "Brutus
and Cassius are traitors, *murderers!* Read us
the will!"

"You really want me to?" said Antony, getting
the paper out again. This was just what he
wanted to happen. "Then come nearer..." Antony
picked up Caesar's cloak, all stained with blood,
and showed them the holes made by the daggers.

"Look," he said, "this was where Brutus stabbed him – Brutus, his best friend. That was what finished Caesar off."

"Traitors! Murderers!" yelled the crowd, and many of them began to weep.

Then Antony told them that Caesar had left all his private estate to the people, along with a sum of money for each of them. At this the crowd went wild. Vowing to avenge Caesar's death, they carried off his body for cremation.

As Antony was congratulating himself on his clever plan, a messenger on horseback galloped up. "Cassius and Brutus have ridden out of the city," he said. "They're lucky to escape alive, the people are so furious..."

*A*ntony and Octavius, Caesar's adopted son, now took command of Rome.

"All the conspirators must die," said Antony ruthlessly. "Brutus and Cassius won't escape, either. They've raised an army, but they'll be no match for us. Tomorrow we march to meet them."

Cassius and Brutus were edgy and afraid. Their great plan had gone terribly wrong and here they were, thrown out of Rome and about to go to battle. They kept arguing about everything, and now a bitter quarrel had broken out about money to pay the troops. All kinds of accusations flew back and forth until they were shouting at the tops of their voices. As usual, it was Cassius who lost his temper and Brutus who tried to calm things down.

"Cassius, we must stop fighting amongst ourselves. We have to make our battle plan. Tomorrow we must face Antony on the plain of Philippi – it's now or never."

Wearily, Brutus went to his tent, but he could not sleep. He kept thinking about the battle to come. The candle flickered and the tent grew darker. Brutus peered into the gloom. He couldn't believe his eyes – the ghost of Julius Caesar was standing before him.

"What do you want?" cried Brutus, his hair standing on end in terror.

The ghost looked straight at him. "You will see me again, Brutus," it said, "at Philippi!"

The following morning the two armies met at Philippi. Both Brutus and Cassius felt a gloomy foreboding. They knew that if they lost the battle, they would rather kill themselves than be taken back to Rome as prisoners.

"Farewell, Cassius," said Brutus, as they put on their armour. "If we never meet again, at least we've parted friends." And with that they went to take up their separate commands.

The battle raged across the plain all day. For a while it seemed that Brutus and Cassius were winning.

But when Cassius looked towards their camp, he saw fires burning. "Antony's troops must be in there!" he cried, and sent his officer Titinius to investigate.

Titinius galloped off and was almost out of sight when he was surrounded by horsemen.

"He's been captured!" shouted a lookout on the hill.

Cassius was horrified and, as always, he saw the worst of things. "So it's all over," he said. "Antony must have won. Oh, what a coward I am, sending my friend to his death like that! There's only one thing left to do now." He called to one of his men and handed him his sword. "Here, this is the sword I killed Caesar with – help me to end it all!"

But just a moment later Titinius came back, unharmed. It had all been a terrible mistake. He looked at Cassius lying dead on the ground and shook his head miserably. "Oh, Cassius, you got it all wrong. It was Brutus who met me – I came back to tell you we were winning! Brutus sent you this wreath of victory, but it doesn't matter now." He put the wreath on Cassius' brow, then picked up Cassius' sword and plunged it into his own heart.

When Brutus arrived and saw the bodies of his friends, he was in despair. "Caesar, your spirit is here as you promised!" he cried. "It's made us bring disaster on ourselves!"

Brutus begged his soldiers to kill him, as Cassius had, but they all refused.

"I know this is the end," he told them. "I have seen the ghost of Caesar again. We can't win, and it's braver to kill ourselves than wait to be captured."

They could hear the sound of Antony's men getting closer and closer, but Brutus would not move. He made one last plea to a soldier called Strato.

"Strato, you're a good man. Hold out your sword and help me."

"Shake hands with me first," said Strato, almost in tears as he picked up the sword.

"Now you can rest, Caesar," murmured Brutus as he fell. "I kill myself more willingly than I killed you."

When Antony and Octavius arrived on the scene, it was all over.

Antony looked down at Brutus' body. "He was the noblest Roman of them all," he said admiringly. "The rest of them killed Caesar because they envied him. Only Brutus acted out of real concern for the people of Rome."

"He will be buried with all honours," promised Octavius. "Now let us go and celebrate this great victory."

The soldiers picked up the bodies of Brutus and Cassius and slowly carried them away. Tomorrow they would return to Rome. The danger was over, and their beloved city would be calm again, safe in the hands of Octavius and Antony.

The Shakespeare Collection

Look out for these other titles in the Shakespeare Collection:

Richard III Retold by James Riordan
Richard, Duke of Gloucester, is a ruthless, ambitious man with only one thing on his mind – he's determined to become King of England. Richard will stop at nothing to secure his destiny, not even cold-blooded murder. Can anyone stand in his way?

King Lear Retold by Anthony Masters
King Lear has set his daughters a test to prove how much they love him. Goneril and Regan flatter the old king, but his youngest daughter, Cordelia, loves him too much to play the game. In a moment of anger, Lear banishes Cordelia. Can any good come out of this rash decision?

As You Like It Retold by Jan Dean
In the magical forest of Arden, it seems, people can catch love like the flu... Celia loves Oliver, Rosalind loves Orlando, and Phebe loves Ganymede. Everything should be perfect. But Ganymede is really Rosalind in disguise, and Orlando has no idea. Will anyone live happily ever after?

You can buy all these books from your local bookseller, or order them direct from the publisher. For more information about The Shakespeare Collection, write to: *The Sales Department, Hodder Children's Books, a division of Hodder Headline Limited, 338 Euston Road, London NW1 3BH.*